Edna's Tale

written & illustrated by
Lisze Bechtold

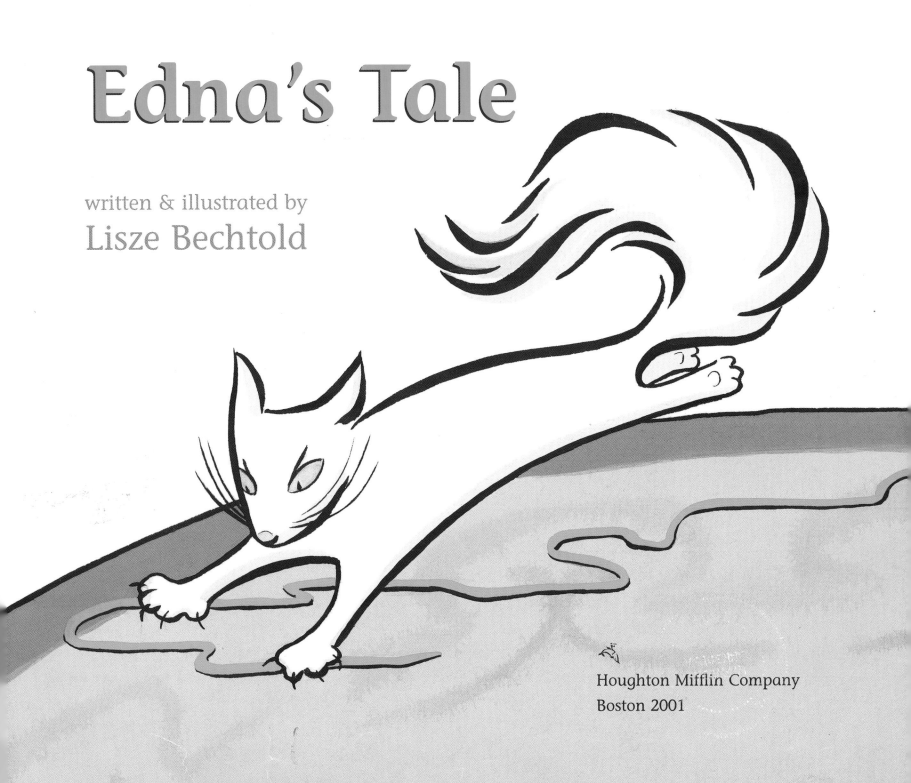

Houghton Mifflin Company
Boston 2001

The text of this book is set in 14.5-point Stone Informal. The illustrations are painted in gouache.

Library of Congress Cataloging-in-Publication Data

Bechtold, Lisze.
Edna's tale / written and illustrated by Lisze Bechtold.
p.   cm.
Summary: Edna, a cat known for her beautiful tail, is in for a couple of surprises when she goes into the woods to meet the new cat in the neighborhood.
ISBN 0-618-09164-5
[1. Cats—Fiction. 2. Tail—Fiction.] I. Title.
PZ7.B380765 Ed 2001
[E]—dc21   00-036945

Manufactured in the United States of America
PHR 10 9 8 7 6 5 4 3 2 1

For my mom, who let me paint big daisies on the family car and her cat, Ivan

Edna had the longest, most fantastically fluffy tail in the neighborhood. She spent every morning licking it clean. Every afternoon she sat at the window so that all the cats in the neighborhood could admire her tail. There was only one thing that was sure to get Edna to go out...

. . . a party.

"It's for everyone to meet the new cat in the neighborhood," Pippa told Edna.

"Come this afternoon to the roof of the house in the woods," added Spike.

"Out in the dirty old woods?" Edna moaned. "All that way?"

But she loved meeting new cats. They always said something nice about her tail.
"Wait until you see the new cat's tail," said Spike slyly. "It's really amazing!"
They dashed off before Edna could ask about it.
They must be tricking me, thought Edna. No one's tail could be more beautiful than mine! But she began to worry. She licked her tail frantically.
Then she got an idea. It was not a pleasant idea, but she knew she had to do it.

Edna ran to the bathroom and gazed at the clutter of beauty supplies.
She emptied the most elegant bottle into the sink.

She cranked on the water,
then gingerly slid into the sink.
The cold water soaked into her fur.
Her skin tingled as towers of
perfumed bubbles
churned around her.

She rinsed

and dried.

Then, for good measure, she spritzed.

"Oooooh," trilled Edna. "No one's tail could be more beautiful than this!"
She stepped outside into the sunlight and strolled proudly down the sidewalk.
As she entered the woods she held her tail high, away from the dusty ground.
Pine needles crunched softly under her paws.
Soon Edna got a quivery feeling, as though she was being followed.

She looked back. "It must have been the butterfly," she told herself, and walked a little faster.

Farther into the woods, the quivery feeling came back.

She sniffed the air, but all she could smell was shampoo.
Edna hurried on.
Suddenly her skin prickled all over.
"I *know* something is following me!" she panted.

She ducked behind a tree.
Listening carefully, she slowly peeked out.

Staring back at her was a horrible, hairy face!

"Aaack!" screamed Edna. She raced up the path with the monster at her heels. She scrambled up a tree and leapt onto a rooftop. The monster followed.

It chased her around and around the chimney.
This monster is never going to give up, thought Edna.
There is only one thing to do.

She spun around and lunged at the monster.

Dust, leaves, and fur went flying as they tumbled across the rooftop.

At last the monster was clamped firmly between Edna's jaws.
"That should teach you!" she growled, her mouth full of fur.

Then Edna looked around. Everyone had arrived for the party, and they were all staring at her. She dropped the monster proudly at her feet. It was streaked with dirt and tangled with leaves. And there was something familiar about it. Something very familiar. It looked very much like...

"My tail!" she cried. "My beautiful tail!" Edna felt weak. Tears stung her eyes.

"Hi, Edna." Pippa giggled. "This is Ivan, the new cat in our neighborhood."

Edna glanced up. "Hello," she whispered.

"I'm so happy to meet you at last," said Ivan. "Everyone told me about your beautiful tail. But no one told me how funny you are!"

"I am?" said Edna. This was something new.

"Would you like to play with me tomorrow?" asked Ivan.

Edna perked up her ears. So what if Ivan's tail was more beautiful than hers.

"You mean, you want to play with me ... anyway?" she asked.

"Of course!" said Ivan. He stood up.

Edna gasped.

"What happened to your tail!" she cried. "Did it fall off?"

"No, no." Ivan laughed. "I was born this way. Haven't you ever heard of a Manx cat?"

"Why yes!" cried Edna. "My great uncle Max was a Manx, too!"

After the party, Edna gave her tail a thorough washing with her tongue. Once again, it was the longest, most fantastically fluffy tail in the neighborhood. But Edna did not sit in the window to be admired—she was too busy gathering all the toys she would take to Ivan's house the next day.

8/2001
$15.00